This book
belongs to:

.................................................

.................................................

To friends of Sayama
Forest, Tryon Creek,
and Belle Isle Marsh.
—P.A.

To mom, dad, Omo,
and Coco for their
love and support.
—A.C.

immedium
inspiring a world of imagination

**Immedium, Inc.**
P.O. Box 31846
San Francisco, CA 94131
www.immedium.com

First hardcover edition published 2012.

Editor: Eric Searleman
Designer: Stefanie Liang

Printed in Malaysia
10 9 8 7 6 5 4 3 2 1

Library of Congress Cataloging-in-Publication Data

Amara, Philip.
 The Treehouse Heroes and the Forgotten Beast /
by Phil Amara ; illustrated by Alina Chau. -- 1st hardcover ed.
    p. cm.
  Summary: "A group of five extraordinary friends and their
teacher help save a magical creature from a tyrannical general"--
Provided by pub.
  ISBN 978-1-59702-034-3 (hardcover)
 [1. Magic--Fiction. 2. Imaginary creatures--Fiction.
3. Conservation of natural resources--Fiction.
4. Superheroes--Fiction.] I. Chau, Alina, ill. II. Title.
 PZ7.A49153Tr 2012
 [E]--dc23
                                              2011052803
ISBN: 978-1-59702-034-3

# The Treehouse
# HEROES
# &The Forgotten Beast

Written by Phil Amara
Illustrated by Alina Chau

immedium • San Francisco, CA

Long ago, in a far-east land,
the *Zez* once roamed free.
Her eyes sparkled like pearls.
Her small paws were white as
snow. Her red fur shimmered
in both sun and starlight.

It was a time of magic creatures, but something was happening to this world.

Villages grew. They chopped, sawed, and shouted.

When old trees fell, the grumbling Yuan left the hills. When rivers dried, the slithering Daidu left the valley.

Now the Zez searched for a new home. All the while, she listened for those who might capture her and use her magic.

When gray clouds gathered over
the canyon, Zez found shelter in
Deep Forest, beyond her meadow.
The storm brought cold and rain.

In the forest, a special tree called to her.
Shaggy moss covered its ancient trunk.
She scampered up the bark when the
lightning frightened her.

This was no
ordinary tree,
but a treehouse!

And, it was no
ordinary home,
but the home of the
Treehouse Heroes.

"I'm Cha, the strongest in the forest," said the muscular new friend.

"I'm Klee the shape-changer," said the young lady. "If you see a mouse, be kind. That's me!"

"I'm Bri," whispered the next boy. "My voice is like the wind. WOOSH!" The lantern's light flickered.

"I'm Flo, and I can vanish before your eyes," said the confident little one. She disappeared with a flash, and reappeared near a glowing lantern.

"I'm Gru, the fastest in the land. I can sprint from here to there," said the boy.

"Are you a Zez?" chirped a voice from another room. "Legend says you are a magical beast."

"This is our Teacher," said Klee, introducing an old man, who carried a cup of tea. "He's trained us to help others..."

"And we're getting good at it!" laughed silly Flo, vanishing again.

"Welcome to our treehouse," the Teacher said calmly.

Soon, the Zez's fur was dry, and the new friends gathered for dinner. Zez enjoyed the lotus seed cake that Gru made. Flo brushed her as she ate.

"Every village had a Zez once," said the Teacher. He told the tale of days when a Zez was a common sight.

"What happened, Teacher?" asked curious Gru.

"General Moon happened," said the Teacher. The heroes shivered at the sound of the villain's name.

"He was a man once, but his enchanted armor changed him. Some say there is no one left inside now," warned the Teacher. "He conquered all the villages, and drove out all the Zez."

"He's not a hero, not even a little," said Bri, cooling his tea with his breath.

"His power grew. But, as each Zez disappeared, each village turned to ruins," said the Teacher, with his furry friend resting on his lap.

"When the Zez is a forgotten beast, things are never the same," cried Cha, plucking a sad note on his lute.

"A wild Zez in a village means the air is cool, and the river is clean. Her presence... her magic ...helps in ways we cannot imagine," said the Teacher.

"Are you really magic, Zez?" asked Flo, watering a potted plant.

Zez licked Flo's face. Placing a white paw on the pot, the plant began to grow! Green shoots stretched from the soil, and flowers appeared like fireworks!

"Again!" giggled Flo.
She held another plant
in a dusty, cracked pot.
The soil was dry as sand.

Zez placed her white paw
on the pot, but this plant
did not grow.

"Zez's magic is only one
part," said the Teacher
to Flo and the rest of
the heroes. "The rest
is up to you."

The next day, the Treehouse Heroes trained.
The Teacher watched.

Cha juggled boulders.

Flo practiced vanishing.

Klee changed into a rabbit,
and hopped through hoops.

Zez dashed with Gru
from rock to rock.

Bri cooled them with
a gentle breeze.
WHOOSH!

"I hope you stay at the treehouse forever,
Zez, and learn new tricks. Forget the meadow.
We're all you need," offered kind Gru.

The Teacher was worried the wild Zez was
becoming too fond of the sweets that Gru
was feeding her.

"What could harm her here?" assured Gru,
tossing her another lotus seed cake.

After dinner, the heroes
rested. Zez licked her
white paws.

When a firefly visited
through the window,
she chased it. When
it flitted to the balcony,
she scooted after it.

Down the tree trunk,
she followed more
dancing lights.

Suddenly, a web of sturdy vines sprung from the shadows! Zez struggled. Her white paws were snared. Then, the net cinched her tight, like a chicken in a pot.

Zez yelped. Gru hurried to the balcony, but saw no Zez. He raced down the tree, tripping on branches, and falling on stones. He found only cake crumbs, tufts of her fur, and the footprints of men.

Klee hoped all was not lost.
Now, in the shape of a fox,
she sniffed out the bandits'
trail. The five friends weaved
their way all night through
Deep Forest. When the
Teacher was tired, he rode
on Cha's shoulders.

In the morning, the zigzag trail ended
at the forest's edge. As fog cleared,
the friends were surprised by what
they saw. Beyond the tree stumps
and mud banks stood a rusty gate.

"This was once Shining River, and home to
wise people," said the Teacher. "They built tall
towers, and from them, saw across the valley.
They lived in harmony with water and wind...
until General Moon came."

"Could magic heal this place?" asked Klee.

"Magic...like our Zez!" exclaimed Flo.
"They brought her here! But where?"

"The tower!" pointed Bri, as his
excited breath stirred a cloud of dust.

Cha summoned his might to open the gates!

Protecting the tower were General Moon's bandits,
who forced the villagers to obey. Behind them,
covered in armor from head to toe, was their leader.

"We've come for our friend!" the heroes called.
But, their foes were already upon them.

Speedy Gru avoided their nets. Sling-stones bounced off of Cha's tough skin. He munched them like nuts.

Bri protected the Teacher. He exhaled a wind that sent the enemy tumbling like leaves.

Flo headed for the tower,
with mouse-size Klee in her
pocket. Invisible, they snuck
by the guards and climbed
the steep stairs of the prison.

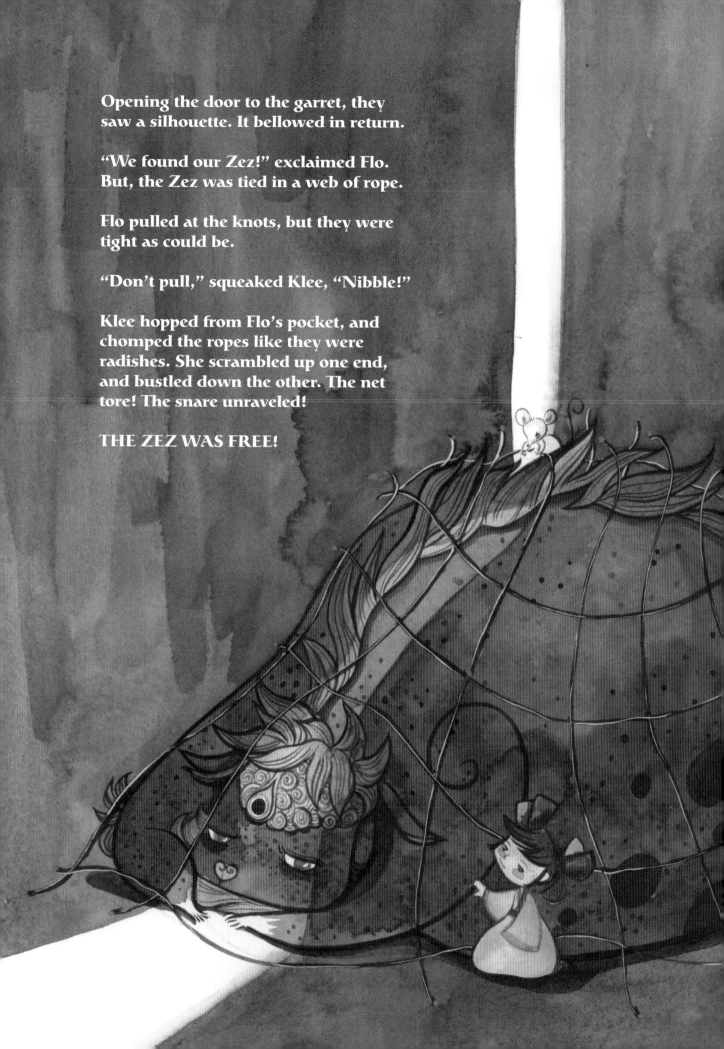

Opening the door to the garret, they saw a silhouette. It bellowed in return.

"We found our Zez!" exclaimed Flo. But, the Zez was tied in a web of rope.

Flo pulled at the knots, but they were tight as could be.

"Don't pull," squeaked Klee, "Nibble!"

Klee hopped from Flo's pocket, and chomped the ropes like they were radishes. She scrambled up one end, and bustled down the other. The net tore! The snare unraveled!

**THE ZEZ WAS FREE!**

With Flo and Klee on her back,
the Zez galloped down the tower
stairs. They saw Cha sitting on a
pile of defeated bandits.

"Stop!" It was General Moon's voice, rumbling
like ten earthquakes. There he stood, invincible
in his dark armor, ready to take back the beast he stole.

"The Zez is mine!" shouted the General. "I will make
her cast my spells! I will use her for my schemes! If this
is the last Zez, I will be its master!"

Cha hurled a boulder, but the General didn't budge. Bri whipped up a windstorm, but the villain stood firm. Gru charged him, and barely dodged his gauntlets.

"Fools!" the General cackled. He stomped toward the frightened Zez, and the ground shook.

When Klee hid under the Teacher's beard, he whispered to her tiny ears. "You can make all the difference," he said, giving Klee confidence.

As Cha's rocks crumbled against the enchanted General, Klee scurried, unnoticed, UNDER the armor plates.

She scratched. She nibbled. She nipped. She climbed up a leg and down an arm. She shimmied all the way to his helmet, and tickled, and tickled, and tickled.

It was more agony than Moon could bear!
He tore off his helmet and tossed it in the mud.
The armor's spell broke! Now, the man inside began
to vanish. A ribbon of smoke evaporated as Moon
expelled one last, ghastly moan.

The once invincible
suit fell to the ground
with a clang.

The Treehouse Heroes wasted no time. Cha retrieved
the helmet and hurled it east. Bri gathered the gauntlets
and blew them west. Gru raced from here to there,
scattering bits of armor in hiding places. Flo and Klee
buried the boots in a secret spot.

The General's henchmen, so startled by the defeat
of their mad leader, ran for the hills in disbelief.

"If General Moon returns, it won't be for a long time,"
said the Teacher.

As the remaining bandits slinked
away, their heads low in shame,
the Zez turned to face them. She
placed her white paws on the trunk
of an old tree. Flowers began to
sparkle and burst on its branches
in rainbow colors.

The tired, hungry
villagers cheered!

"With the Zez's magic all around us, Shining River will be lush once more!" smiled a villager.

"The Zez is ours!" added another.

"It's not your choice to keep her here," said Cha.

"And, magic alone won't save this place," added Bri. "Care for Shining River, and the Zez will want to stay."

The heroes hugged Zez one last time.

Before she trotted past the gate,
the Zez looked back to her friends
and the villagers. Then, she dashed
into the wilderness, continuing her
search for a new, unspoiled home.

"Her magic is only one part..."
said the Teacher.

Flo remembered
her potted plants
back at the treehouse.
She held her Teacher's
hand and added,
"...the rest is
up to you."